Welcome to the world of Lucas, Jake and Amber.
Join them on an adventure where they arrive at
Harland and Wolff in Belfast just minutes before
the Titanic is about to sail.

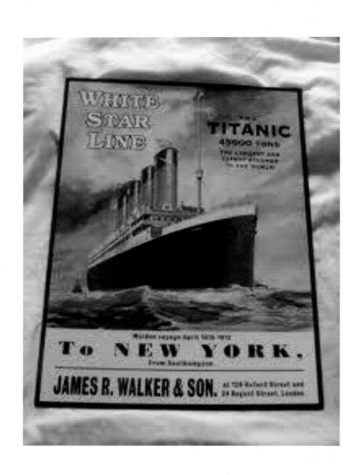

This book is dedicated to my family.

Launch

OF

White Star Royal Mail Triple-Screw Steamer

"TITANIC"

At BELFAST,

Wednesday, 31st May, 1911, at 12-15 p.m.

Admit Bearer.

Email: jjsmyth1@hotmail.com
Website: www.JimmySmythAuthor.com

Titanic: The Untold Story

Written by: Jimmy Smyth

Illustrated by: Ozzy Esha

Lucas' mother and father had been planning a trip to Belfast to visit the Titanic exhibition, in the new Titanic Centre. Lucas had been reading about it for some time and couldn't wait to go and see it. Finally the day arrived and Lucas, Jake and Amber piled into the backseat of the car. Jake kept himself very busy sniffing at the seats and carpet, while Amber sat in Lucas' lap and stared out the window.

To anyone driving by, they looked like a normal boy and his dogs; but this couldn't be further from the truth.

They had extraordinary adventures. Jake and Amber had been given magical powers by a leprechaun, whose life they had saved. Amber had the ability to talk and to swim like a fish. Jake had the ability to run faster and jump higher than any other dog and Lucas had a special gold medallion, with a hole in the centre that allowed them to travel back in time.

But today they were just a little boy and his two dogs, and very excited about seeing a new exhibition. When they arrived at Titanic Belfast they all jumped out of the car. They had to be careful to hide their magical abilities from other people, even from Lucas' Mum and Dad.

"Oh dear," his Mum said as she read a sign outside of the exhibit. "They do not allow dogs inside," she frowned. She knew that Lucas would be very disappointed. Lucas was sad, but Jake and Amber were even sadder.

They hung their heads as they sat on the pavement.

"It's okay Lucas," his father said. "You can stay here with Jake and Amber while we go take a look and then I will stay here with the dogs, while you and Mum visit the exhibition. Does that sound okay?" Lucas nodded but he was still very sad. He knew that Jake and Amber were just as excited as he was. "Don't worry," he whispered to them as he crouched down beside them. "I will tell you all about it."

Jake and Amber tried not to show how sad they were and licked Lucas' hands. Lucas could tell they were still upset, but he thought for a moment, until he came up with an idea. Jake and Amber could not go inside but maybe there was a window where they could all peek inside. Lucas walked around the back of the building and Jake and Amber followed closely after.

Lucas had just spotted a window that he thought might give them a good view, when Jake began crouching and growling. He was looking at someone standing half in the shadows. "It's okay," Lucas reassured Jake with a pat on his head.

"He is just looking for a few coppers." Lucas could see that the man was in his sixties or seventies. Just then they heard some commotion behind them. It was a flock of seagulls that had gathered and they were being very noisy. When Lucas turned back, the old man was gone.

When Lucas tried to look in the window they found, there was nothing to see. So the three decided it was time for a snack. Lucas dug into his pocket to see if he had enough money left to buy some sweets. He found that there was only one coin left in his pocket. When he pulled it out, he realised it was not a coin at all.

It was the magical medallion that the ghostly monk had given him, the day that Jake, Amber, and he visited the ancient monastery. That day they had been able to travel through time, and experience what it was like in the past. Lucas held up the medallion and looked through the hole in the middle of it.

Suddenly a heavy mist descended and surrounded them. Jake and Amber started barking. They could not see through the mist and it was a little frightening. Lucas could not look away from the hole in the medallion. He could see on the other side of it a boy, about seventeen years old, walking toward him. As the mist disappeared, the boy was getting closer and closer to Lucas until he was standing right in front of him. Lucas felt very strange and a little bit dizzy.

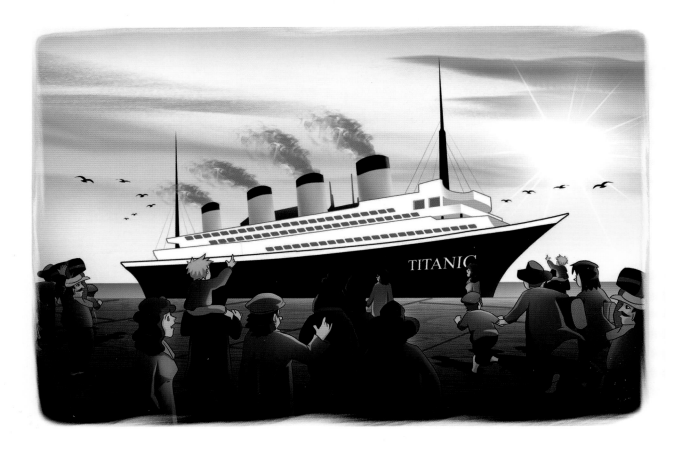

In the distance behind the boy, was the most magnificent ship he had ever seen. It was tall and very large and there were hundreds of people in strange looking clothing, standing nearby. The ladies wore long dresses and the men, old fashioned suits. Some of the ladies wore large floppy hats, and some of the men wore tall top hats. Everyone was chattering and very excited about their journey on the ship.

"Hello," the boy said to Lucas, with a friendly smile. "Hello," Lucas replied, still feeling strange. He was starting to understand that they had once again travelled into the past. The boy reached down to pat Jake and Amber and the dogs licked at his hands happily. "My name is Jack Harper," he said as he stood back up. "Are you sailing on the ship?"

Lucas's mind was still spinning as he tried to figure out where they were, or more importantly, when. "My name is Lucas," he said, "and this is Jake, and Amber." Lucas glanced past Jack at the ship again. "Is that why everyone is here, to sail on that ship?" Lucas asked, still awed by how beautiful the ship was. "Oh yes," Jack said quickly. "But not just any ship," he grinned as they walked closer to the ship. "This is the greatest ship ever built, the Titanic!"

Lucas was stunned as he noticed the similarity between the ship and the pictures he had seen. The pictures could never show just how magnificent and awesome the ship was. Now that he was actually seeing it with his own eyes, he understood the excitement.

"This is its maiden voyage," Jack said, his eyes wide with excitement. "The very first trip it will take." He lowered his voice to a whisper and leaned close to Lucas as he added, "Can you believe it? I will be sailing on the Titanic? I was one of the apprentices that worked on the ship, and I got picked to go along on its very first voyage!" he sighed with amazement.

Lucas' mind was racing. He could see that Jack was very excited and that he had no idea what tragedy awaited the Titanic.

"Well aren't you afraid of getting seasick?" Lucas asked. His heart was pounding. "Don't you worry about falling off the ship?" Jack laughed and shook his head. "Oh no, I can't wait!" With that he started to hurry off, leaving Lucas, Jake, and Amber to stare after him.

There was no one else nearby so Amber spoke up, using her magical ability to speak human. "Stop him Lucas! That ship is going to sink," she said and pranced back and forth nervously. "I know," said Lucas. "But what can we do?" He sighed sadly as he realised that there was nothing they could do to prevent the tragedy.

Maybe they could at least stop one person from perishing. He began to run after Jack, with Jake and Amber close behind him.

"Stop, Jack!" Lucas called. Jack glanced over his shoulder, and then stopped. He frowned when he saw how upset Lucas looked. 'What's wrong?" he asked. "Jack, I can't explain it, but you should not get on that ship. It will sink!" Lucas hoped Jack would believe him. Instead Jack laughed. "The Titanic is the safest ship ever built! It is unsinkable! You should not worry so much," he insisted.

Lucas sighed heavily as he realised that Jack was not going to listen to him. To Jack the Titanic was the safest place to be. The only other thing that Lucas could think of was to somehow distract Jack. He noticed a silver chain sticking out of Jack's pocket. "What is that?" Lucas asked, hoping to keep Jack's mind away from Titanic.

Jack pulled the chain from his pocket and revealed that it was a silver pocket watch. He turned it over to show Lucas the engraving on the back. It said: Jack Harper Titanic 1912 "This is a special gift from my parents. They saved for over a year in order to buy this watch for me," he beamed proudly.

"Oh where did they buy it?" Lucas asked slyly, knowing that Jack might miss the ship if Lucas kept his attention. "Not sure," Jack replied. Then he noticed the time the watch was showing. "Oh no, I'll miss the ship if I don't hurry." Lucas reluctantly gave the watch back to Jack, and Jack quickly put the watch back in his pocket.

"Wait!" Lucas said as Jack was turning away. "Could you please tell me where the toilets are?" he asked urgently. Jack frowned as he did not want to be late, but he could tell that Lucas needed to go to the toilet urgently.

"Alright," he said with a nod. "Follow me," he started down the dock. "Hurry, I have only a few minutes to get on the ship." He gestured for them to move faster.

Lucas, Jake, and Amber followed Jack into an enormous building. Lucas was amazed by the size of it, and wondered what it was used for. "What is this place?" he asked. "This is Harland and Wolff's drawing office," he explained. "This is where the plans for the Titanic were drawn up."

The building was empty, as everyone had rushed out onto the dock to wave goodbye to the Titanic. Jack kept looking toward the door and Lucas knew it would take something drastic to keep him from getting on the ship. He looked around for anything that might help them protect Jack. That was when he noticed that there were large wooden cupboards on both sides of the drawing office and the doors of the cupboards had locks and keys.

"Hurry, hurry," Jack urged as they neared the toilets. Lucas noticed that one of the cupboards was wide open and the key was still in the door. He quickly turned around to Jake and Amber and whispered, "Be ready." Lucas jumped as if he was frightened by something. "Jack!" he pointed to the cupboard shakily. "Something moved in there!"

Jack muttered, "Probably just a rat," and walked over to take a closer look. When he stuck his head into the cupboard to see what might be hiding, Lucas nodded at Jake and as quick as lightening, Jake jumped into the air and with his front paws stretched out, he gave Jack's back a solid push. Jack cried out as he tumbled into the cupboard. Lucas, Jake, and Amber all pushed the cupboard door shut together and Lucas snapped the lock into place.

Jack began frantically banging on the door. "Please! Let me out!" he begged, as he struck the wooden doors as hard as he could. "Please Lucas, if you don't, I will miss my dream of going to New York on the Titanic! Why are you doing this to me?" he cried.

Lucas stepped back from the cupboard a little worried that Jack might be able to break it open. "I'm sorry Jack," he said sadly. "I can't let you out. In a few days, you will understand why."

Lucas was happy that he could protect Jack, but as he heard the ship sound its horn, he was sad that he could not protect the other passengers. Lucas, Jake, and Amber hurried toward the drawing office door. They could still hear Jack shouting and banging on the cupboard door. He was very, very, angry.

"Run as fast as you can!" Lucas told Jake and Amber. "We don't want anyone catching us. They would make us let Jack out."

As they rushed through the door Lucas noticed that there was a large key in the outer door, so he locked the outer door and removed the key. Jake ran ahead as he was the fastest. He got as close to the Titanic as he could and Amber was right behind him. Lucas took the cupboard key and the door key out of his pocket and held them in his palm. "We can't let anyone find these until long after the ship has left," he said softly. Amber lifted her head. "Give them to me Lucas and I will make sure they can't be found." Lucas held the keys out and Amber took them gently between her teeth. She jumped off the dock and into the water causing a small splash.

No one noticed as they were all waving to the people on the ship. People were shouting, some were singing and there was a band playing music. Everyone was very excited. Amber swam out to the middle of the dock and deep down to the bottom of the water. She wedged the keys beneath some rocks. She could see the bottom of the Titanic and it was massive. Quickly Amber swam upward and joined Lucas and Jake on the dock.

Lucas had tears in his eyes as he watched the ship begin to pull away. They had been able to save Jack, which was wonderful, but he wished that he could have done more.

"Let's go," said Lucas sadly, as Jake and Amber bowed their heads. Lucas had been fascinated by the ship before, but now he understood just how powerful this moment in history was. No one had expected what was to come, in the days ahead.

Jake and Amber followed closely behind Lucas, until he arrived at the spot where he had met the old man. He held up the golden medallion and stared through it once again. Soon he could see people walking around outside of the exhibition. They wore modern clothing. A thick mist surrounded them once more, and Jake and Amber began to bark nervously.

As the mist lifted, Lucas spotted his Mum and Dad, who were just coming out of the Titanic exhibition. His Mum was wiping a tear from her eye. "Alright Lucas," his Dad said. "Now it's your turn to go in. You will really love the Titanic exhibition" "No thanks," Lucas said quietly. "I have seen enough for one day."

His mother and father exchanged looks of amazement, as Lucas had talked for months about visiting the exhibition. "Well alright," his Mum said. "If you really don't want to go in, then we will head back home." She patted Lucas' shoulder lightly. They all began to walk to the car together and as they got near their car, the old man waved to Lucas. Lucas' Dad noticed him.

"Here Lucas, give that man some change." He handed Lucas the change from his pocket. Lucas nodded and took it to the old man, with Jake and Amber trailing behind. When the old man looked up he had an enormous smile on his face. He patted the dogs gently and accepted the change from Lucas.

"My father used to spend all of his free time here, waiting to find a young boy and his two dogs," he said, as he looked from Lucas to Jake then towards Amber. Lucas' eyes widened as he realised that the man he was now talking to must be Jack's son.

The old man lowered his voice as he knew that their adventures must be kept a secret. "He always believed that you three would come back here and before he died he asked me to come here, to thank you."

He looked at Lucas with gratitude. "Were it not for the three of you, I would not be here today; so thank you. Thank you for saving the life of my father, Jack Harper."

Lucas was astounded. He had never considered that Jack would have children. By saving one life he had really saved an entire family. Lucas glanced up when he heard his parents' car pulling up behind him. "Are you ready Lucas?" his father asked. The old man handed Lucas a small bag and this made Lucas' stomach rumble, as he thought that the bag contained some chocolates . "That's for you," the old man said, his eyes sparkling. "Thank you," said Lucas. Lucas started to run off, then he paused to look back. "Goodbye, it was nice meeting you!" He gave a final wave to the old man and the old man waved back.

When Lucas, Jake, and Amber, were settled in the backseat of the car Lucas opened the paper bag. He wanted to share some of the chocolates that the old man had given him with his parents. When he opened the bag, there was something that glimmered in the sunlight that was shining through the car window. He reached in and pulled it out. It was a silver chain with an old pocket watch at the end. Lucas turned the watch over and discovered an engraving on the back: Jack Harper Titanic 1912.

Lucas held the watch tightly in his hand as Jake and Amber laid their heads against his knees. They were all very happy that Jack had been saved and they spent the car journey home quietly remembering yet another wonderful adventure.

About The Author

I grew up in a small town called Kilkeel, situated between the mountains and the sea, right in the heart of The Kingdom of Mourne: a place that has never ceased to captivate me, by its magic and beauty.

My grandmother and many of her neighbours were great storytellers and hardly a week went by without a storytelling session. Many of the stories were about the fairies and had a local setting and in the days following, my friends and I would be playing in the fields or by the river where the stories took place.

Each week I would be at the newsagents, an hour early, waiting on the Dandy and Beano to arrive. When I got my copy, I was so excited that I just wanted to jump straight into the world of comic land. I couldn't even wait a few minutes until I ran three hundred yards to my granny's house; so instead, I just lay down on the pavement outside the newsagent's, spread out the comic and disappeared into the world of Desperate Dan, Korky the Cat and the rest of their friends.

It was magic.

Other books and audio books by the author:

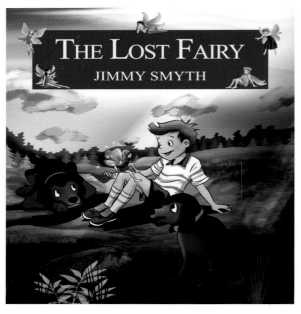